THE
DEAD
DETECTIVE

IN

SIX FEET UNDER

THE
DEAD
DETECTIVE

IN

SIX FEET UNDER

by Felix Bogarte™

Published 2003 by Books Noir Ltd, Glasgow

Copyright © 2003 Books Noir Ltd

Text written by Joan Love and Mhairi MacDiarmid,
based on a story by Mhairi MacDiarmid

A CIP catalogue for this book is available from the British Library

ISBN 1-904684-01-7

Printed and bound in the EU

www.booksnoir.com
www.deaddetective.com
info@deaddetective.com

CONTENTS

WHO'S WHO IN
DEAD DETECTIVE LAND

WHO IS CHARLIE CHRISTIAN?

12 year-old Charlie Christian is a born detective – and has been given the opportunity to prove himself. The Court Of Ghouls, who exist in a twilight zone between life and death have decreed that the Dead Detective, Hank Kane be sentenced to fight crime in Charlie's very own city of Glasgow! And, as Hank Kane cannot be trusted to solve cases honestly he has been instructed to take on someone he can train as a detective – someone like Charlie Christian.

WHO IS THE GRIM REAPER?

The Grim Reaper, or TG as he likes to be known, really enjoys his work. He loves the perks of his job, annoying Hank, partying and fiddling his expenses.

SO, WHO IS THE DEAD DETECTIVE?

The Dead Detective is Hank Kane, a crooked cop, killed in the line of duty in Los Angeles in the 1950s. Instead of passing straight over to the other side, however, Hank finds himself facing the Court Of Ghouls, who have decided that he'll have to pay for his habit of planting evidence on suspects. They sentence him to fighting crime, using only honest methods, until they are convinced that he's learnt his lesson. They instruct The Grim Reaper to keep an eye on Hank. It isn't that they don't totally trust Hank – it's just that they don't trust him at all!

Hank's other problem is his appearance. He's a skeleton! During daylight hours he has no flesh on his bones (well, he *is* dead!) and so has to stay out of sight. At night, however, providing he drinks some of his chemical compound, flesh returns to his bones and he looks almost normal. "Almost" because Hank died fifty years previously and has been catapulted forward in time to 2003.

CHAPTER ONE
DOWN AND OUT

THE man was dressed in black from head to toe. He pushed open the door very gently but it still creaked ever so slightly. He stopped and listened, waiting for a sign that someone had heard. Nothing. He stepped inside, his eyes adjusting quickly to the darkness.

He knew instantly that he'd made a mistake. The room was full of nothing but junk. Old furniture, old paintings, old wallpaper, old smells. Nothing expensive at all. He peered at a photograph on the desk. An autographed picture of Joe Di Maggio. Big deal. Beside it was an unusual shaped bottle with a picture of a skull and crossbones on it. He picked it up and sniffed the top of it. It stank.

In the semi-darkness he struggled with three big and bulky objects. He moved them aside and almost tripped over a large rug on the floor. He placed the rug very carefully over the three objects. He knew he had precious little time here. He didn't want to get caught in an office that wasn't his. He'd have trouble explaining that at this time of night.

He crept over to the large office desk and began opening drawers quietly, always listening for a sign that someone was aware of his presence. He took a small torch from his pocket and began to examine the contents of one of the drawers. A notebook, a couple of pencils, a half empty packet of gum. But there, hidden right at the back of the drawer was a wallet.

He took it from its hiding place and saw that it was full of notes. He pulled a few out. Dollars? The wallet was full of dollars. He pushed the drawer closed. This guy must be planning a trip to the States soon, he thought. He made a quick decision to take the wallet anyway. He shoved it inside his jacket and made his way back across the room. He was startled when a door just off the main office opened. The light from the room revealed the figure of Hank Kane.

"Hey, just what d'you think you're doing, buddy?" yelled Hank as the intruder ran for the door.

"Stay right where you are!" shouted Hank as the man made a hasty exit and ran down the stairs. Hank grabbed his hat from the hat-stand (he never went anywhere without it) and followed the man. Hank could see the intruder at the bottom of the stairs. The man turned to look back up at Hank, then pushed open the door which led out onto Gordon Street.

By the time Hank got out onto the street, the man had disappeared from sight. Hank looked quickly in both directions and made a split decision to go right. It was two o'clock in the morning so there were very few people on the streets. Those who were strolling by couldn't help taking a second look at the weird guy running down the street.

It had been raining heavily all night but Hank was

getting used to the weather. After all, he'd been living in Glasgow for some time now, and a day *without* rain was unusual.

He turned right into Buchanan Street. Suddenly he spotted the burglar in the distance. He picked up speed and gave chase.

"Hey!" he shouted. "Get back here, buddy, you and I got some unfinished business."

The rain was running down the street, creating fast moving streams in the gutters. Hank was concentrating so much on watching the burglar that he didn't notice the rising water, until it made him lose his footing. He slipped and tried in vain to steady himself. He fell to the ground, his head making contact with a large concrete litterbin. The blood gushed from his wound and for a few seconds the rainwater which swirled around him was stained red.

The burglar saw him fall and heaved a sigh of relief. He slowed his pace completely and began to walk along Argyle Street. He'd just got away with another crime, unscathed!

In the meantime, Hank had lost consciousness. He lay, face down, in the middle of the street with the relentless rain pouring down on him. The few passers-by who did see him thought he was a drunk and immediately crossed over to the other side of the road. If they'd looked more closely they'd have noticed that the "drunk's" skin was falling from his bones.

CHAPTER TWO

DISAPPEARING ACT

IT WAS exactly nine o'clock on Saturday morning when Charlie Christian arrived outside Hank's office, in Gordon Street. Hank had phoned the day before and asked him to come over.

Charlie hadn't expected to hear from Hank Kane ever again. After they'd solved the "Jackson Case" Hank had said his goodbyes to Charlie and his sister, Annie, making it clear that their partnership was over. Charlie had formed the distinct impression that Hank was on his way out of the city, out of the country, out of his life, forever.

The day after the case was solved, Charlie had gone to Hank's office intending to plead for at least one last case. But when he got to Gordon Street, instead of finding Hank's office, all he'd found was a boarded up building, with no doorways or windows. He'd run into McColl's newsagent nearby and asked where Kane Investigations had moved to. Olivia, the girl behind the till, knew Charlie well as he bought all his detective magazines there.

"What 'Investigations'?" she'd asked.

"Hank Kane, from along the road. You know, the detective agency."

"Charlie, what are you on about?" She really had no idea who or what Hank Kane was.

"The office was right there," said Charlie, pointing down the road.

"What's your scam, Charlie?" Olivia asked, coming out to the doorway. "There's never been an office there. There isn't even a doorway."

"See that wall," Charlie persisted, "the one with the posters all over it? Are you telling me you've never seen a doorway there?"

"No, I've never seen a doorway there," repeated Olivia, getting annoyed.

"And you've never heard of Kane Investigations?" asked Charlie again.

"Look, Charlie," said Olivia, going back to the till, "I've got work to do. I've no time for messing about." That poor kid's lost the plot, she thought. Totally wrapped up in some loony story. Charlie left the newsagents in a very confused state.

He'd checked a few times since then and found the same wall with the posters on it but no doorway. He'd even tried tapping the wall to see if the doorway was hidden behind the posters. He eventually gave up when people walking by started asking him if he was blind.

He'd taken his sister Annie with him and even she'd confessed to being stumped. And this was not a confession she made often and certainly not to her brother! She had finally dragged Charlie away from the wall, saving him from possible ridicule but only because she didn't want to be defamed by association.

They had talked about it since, but Annie had simply moved on with her life, while Charlie began to doubt the whole episode had happened at all.

So when the call came from Hank, not only did it provide Charlie with an opportunity to quiz Hank on his invisible office but also to once again exercise his detective skills. Whereas his sister Annie would, upon receiving a call from Hank Kane, immediately think of words like "danger" or "life-threatening", Charlie could only hear "adventure", or "glory".

Besides, he'd been curious as to why he'd never met Hank during the daytime – it had always been at night, at Hank's insistence. Charlie was also very curious about Hank himself, a guy who looked like he'd stepped out of a Bogart movie, who was so unfamiliar with the things everyone else took for granted and whose office had simply disappeared! Very weird, Charlie had thought.

The fact that the office was there at all this morning was confusing. Charlie felt like dragging Olivia from McColl's to show her the doorway but something told him to check things out with Hank first. Hank might, just might, explain his mysterious existence to *Charlie* (he *had* called him, after all) – but not to the whole world.

Charlie had rung the doorbell twice now but there was no reply. He stepped back and looked up towards the window. Nothing. He took his mobile phone from his pocket and keyed in Hank's number.

He let it ring for what seemed like an eternity but there was no reply.

He pressed the doorbell again and waited. Still nothing. Charlie suddenly realised that he was hungry. Having rushed out with no breakfast, he decided to go and get something to eat and come back in about an hour.

He left a note for Hank, just so as he could prove that at least *he'd* been on time! Imagine being forced to get up to go and meet someone who couldn't keep the appointment, thought Charlie. He had a real problem with that, this being a Saturday and all.

Meanwhile, Hank was having some problems of his own!

*   *   *   *   *   *   *

When daylight had come and the town began to wake up, Hank's decomposing body was still lying in Buchanan Street.

A road sweeper, named Pete Smith, had been the first to spot him. At first he thought Hank was just another homeless down-and-out on the streets of Glasgow then, on closer inspection, he realised with a shock that the guy was dead. And what's more he looked like the remains of something out of a horror movie!

He called the police and by the time they arrived, a small crowd of onlookers had gathered. They stood and stared curiously at the skeleton draped in old-fashioned clothes, a hat lying by his side.

"I thought you said it was a body you'd found," remarked PC Murray to Pete, when he arrived on the scene.

"It was," replied Pete, "but it decomposed in the time it took you guys to get here!"

"That's almost funny, Pete,'' said PC Murray.

"But I'm not joking! I'm telling you, that skeleton wasn't a skeleton when I called you, honest!"

PC Murray knew Pete was an honest man. The local police had relied on Pete for many years and were amazed at the information he'd come across while sweeping the streets over the past twenty years.

Although PC Murray had only been in the force for three years, he'd discovered very early in his career just how much the local police relied on people like Pete. They were the people who were in the city every day, cleaning up after the masses of workers, tourists and revellers had messed up the streets yet again and left the likes of Pete to clean up after them.

Around seven o'clock each morning, Pete often watched the first commuters spill out of Central Station onto his streets with the first wave of litter appearing as they left. Empty coffee cups, full coffee cups, chocolate bar wrappers, half eaten sausage rolls; all thrown onto his streets. And the next day, when this vast messy monster of a crowd re-emerged from the station, it never wondered how the streets had got so clean since it last fowled them up.

But, sometimes among the daily litter, as well as the odd item of interest (or of value), were clues left by careless criminals. Criminals who, like everyone else, were unaware that someone had to sift through their rubbish.

"Someone must know something. Someone must have placed the body there," Pete was saying to another policeman. "A body can't decompose as quickly as that and he definitely wasn't there yesterday."

It was a mystery, there was no doubt about that. But the crowd on the street was getting larger and noisier and PC Murray and his colleague knew they had to get the body off the street as soon as possible. They radioed for help and pretty soon an ambulance arrived. The remains were lifted carefully onto a stretcher, placed inside the ambulance and driven to the nearest morgue.

Pete's day seemed very dull after the skeleton had gone.

CHAPTER THREE

THE ENVELOPE

IN THE meantime, Charlie, full of sugary doughnuts and coca-cola, was on his way back to Hank's office. He tried the handle of the outer door, expecting to find that it was still locked but was pleasantly surprised to find that it now opened. He quickly climbed the stairs to Hank's office and found *that* door, too, was open. Now *that's* unusual, thought Charlie, Hank was always pretty careful about security.

As soon as he saw the inside of the office he knew something was wrong. The room was in complete disarray. A lamp had been knocked over and lay on the floor. The drawer in Hank's desk lay open, the contents were muddled and a wad of dollars lay on the floor. What kind of burglar would leave money? he thought.

Charlie went into the small side room where Hank slept. It was empty. His bed didn't look as though it had been slept in. He went back to the main office and checked the hat stand. It too was empty.

Charlie didn't know what to do. Should he call the police? No. He knew, instinctively, that Hank wouldn't want him to do that. He looked around Hank's desk for clues; a note, anything.

Hank kept a notebook and pencil beside his

telephone and Charlie began to thumb through it, looking for something that would help. Hank's scribbles were almost illegible and Charlie couldn't find anything of interest.

He sat back in Hank's chair and looked around the office again. A picture on the wall was slightly askew and Charlie also noticed an ashtray had been overturned. There were two keys inside the opened desk drawer and Charlie took them out and looked at them curiously. He stood up and tried them in the office door. One of them was the right size but he wondered what the other key was for.

He tried Hank's bedroom door but the key was too big. The desk drawer didn't have a lock. He fingered the key thoughtfully and looked around the room. His eyes came to rest on a small wooden bureau underneath the window. He crossed the room quickly, put the key in the lock and turned it. Success! The bureau opened and Charlie looked inside.

A small white envelope was all the bureau held and Charlie lifted it gingerly. Written in bold, black, letters were the words:

ONLY TO BE OPENED IN AN EMERGENCY

Charlie took the envelope back to the desk and decided that this situation had to be an emergency. He pulled up the chair and opened the envelope. Somehow, he knew he was going to be in for a long read.

"Dear Charlie," the letter began, *"If you have opened this letter then something has obviously gone very wrong and I'm probably gonna need your help to put things right. But first of all, I think I have some explaining to do."*

As Charlie read on, his eyes grew wider and wider in disbelief. In the letter, Hank explained everything. Unbelievable as he knew it would seem, he told Charlie the whole, incredible story of how he was actually dead. He told him about the Court of Ghouls and how they wouldn't allow him to "cross over to the other side" till he solved a case honestly. He told him all about the skull and crossbones medicine – the chemical compound that allowed his flesh to return to his bones. The medicine that, in the hours of darkness at least, allowed him to look almost normal.

Reluctant though Charlie was to accept what the letter said, parts of it were beginning to make sense. It explained why Hank seemed to be stuck in a time warp; how he never ventured out during the day and his complete ignorance of all things technical.

Charlie had guessed from his first meeting with Hank Kane that something weird was going on. Now he actually felt a little satisfaction from having already realised that Hank was some sort of ghost. It heightened his sense of adventure. "I'm one helluva detective, ain't I?" he muttered to himself as he turned the page and read on.

"Also inside this envelope are details of our current case,

which you'll need to solve. I'll need you to find out what's happened to me, too. Hope you're up to the job, Kid."

Charlie screwed up his face. He hated when Hank called him "Kid". He tried to ignore it and moved on to the next paragraph.

"Finally," continued Hank, *"And I'm sorry to give you yet another shock, I have to tell you that I have someone else who occasionally does a bit of leg work for me. Only problem is, Kid, that he's kinda, well, dead too. I know, I know…"* Charlie could almost hear him speaking the words, *"…this thing's just getting weirder and weirder.*

"The Court of Ghouls didn't trust me to solve cases honestly, you see, so they sent someone to keep an eye on me. His name's TG (short for The Grim Reaper).

"He's okay, really, you'll like him once you get to know him. Thinks he's a bit of a cool dude. You'll know how to play him I'm sure – you both have the same mental age I guess. Don't let the robes or the scythe put you off, kid, underneath it all he's a pussycat."

Charlie stopped reading. "Scythe? Robes? Pussycat?" he wondered aloud. What was Hank talking about?

While he'd been reading the letter, he'd been aware of a strange, rotting smell and it now suddenly grew stronger. He looked up.

The Grim Reaper materialised from nowhere and now stood, dark and terrifying, in the middle of the office. His black cloak covered him from head to toe and his right hand clutched a huge scythe. Just visible beneath the hood of his cloak were his staring, red eyes, which seemed to burn into Charlie's very soul.

He reached out his left hand towards Charlie who dropped the letter and surrendered himself to pure terror.

CHAPTER FOUR

DUST TO DUST

Baird Street Police Station, Glasgow

FORENSICS had been called in and had carried out their examination. The guy they were looking at had been murdered about fifty years ago. They'd managed to find an old bullet wound and reckoned that was the cause of death.

What they couldn't explain was why somebody had suddenly decided to dump his remains on the street. Whoever had done that, had some explaining to do.

Poor guy, thought PC Murray, as he looked at the skeleton, he'd never even been given a proper funeral. The local police decided to organise one. Once they'd checked that he didn't match any of their open missing persons' files, they arranged for Hank Kane's remains to be buried that day.

*   *   *   *   *   *   *

The closing strains of *The Lord's My Shepherd* rang out in the almost empty church. Hank's coffin was in front of the altar. PC Murray and his colleague folded their hymn sheets and sat down. The priest cleared his throat and said a few words.

The body was taken from the church and the gravediggers took over. A plot had been chosen and a hole dug in readiness. The coffin was slowly lowered into the ground just as the first drops of rain began to fall. The two police officers replaced their hats and moved away towards their car. One of the gravediggers picked up his spade and threw the first sprinkling of soil on top of the coffin.

Six feet under, Hank, a powerless skeleton, heard the soil hit the wooden box.

CHAPTER FIVE
THE REAPER

CHARLIE leaned as far back in Hank's chair as he could, without falling over.

The Grim Reaper! The Grim Reaper was in the same room as him! But this guy only showed up when someone was about to die! Charlie was more than a little frightened and it showed!

TG began to speak, his fetid breath filling the room as he did so.

"It's okay, Charlie, I haven't come for you. Your time's not up, just yet," he chuckled.

He leant his scythe against the wall and pulled up a chair. Charlie pinched himself. This just had to be a dream, no, make that a nightmare. Any minute now, he'd wake up and find himself back home in his bedroom.

"I know this must be a real shock for you, Charlie, but you've read Hank's letter by now and you can see he's in trouble. It's up to you and I to help him."

"H...h... how do you know my name?" Charlie stammered, trying desperately to compose himself.

"I know everything about you Charlie," TG replied. "I've been working with Hank from the beginning, from the first time you stepped through the door. It was just that he felt perhaps you weren't quite ready to meet me. However, certain events have forced me to introduce myself."

What an understatement, thought Charlie. He glanced down at the letter again, written in Hank's familiar scrawl. The words danced on the page. Charlie was too warm and he badly needed a drink of cool water. However, he knew if he tried to stand his legs would just buckle underneath him.

TG cleared his throat. "Look, pal, so you've had your fright for the day, big deal. Glad we've got that over with. Have you any idea just how boring it is for me? Day in, day out, I've got to humour schmucks who meet me for the first time. There, there, I say. Like, I care.

"Hank was different, I'll give him that. Guess that's why I have a soft spot for him, even if he does drive me crazy at times. Anyway Kid…you don't mind if I call you 'Kid' do you?"

"Would it matter if I did?" asked Charlie in a slightly trembling voice.

"No," replied TG. He looked at Charlie and smiled. "Hey, you know something, you remind me of Hank. And that means we're gonna get along just fine."

Charlie forced himself to meet TG's eyes for the first time and felt his courage return, if only slightly. At least, his plan had changed from running screaming from the building to listening to what TG had to say. The fact that he had absolutely no choice in the matter played a small part in Charlie's decision!

The Grim Reaper rested his elbow on the desk and the sleeve of his cloak rode up to reveal long, bony arms attached to skeletal fingers. He continued speaking. "I wasn't here in the early hours of the morning when Hank was burgled. I was on my way home from the local nightclub..."

Charlie's eyes widened as TG continued.

"I saw Hank running down Buchanan Street in pursuit of someone. Judging from the mess of the office I can only assume that the guy he was chasing was a burglar. Anyway, Hank fell and knocked himself unconscious. As I think he explained in his letter, if he doesn't drink his compound he returns to his skeletal form and so obviously, when the police found him, they assumed he was dead. Only you and I know different."

Charlie straightened in his chair. Though the whole situation was completely bizarre, his naturally inquisitive mind had taken over and he couldn't help but be interested in what The Grim Reaper had to say. He had one important question and found enough courage to ask it.

"If you saw all this, why didn't you help him? Why didn't you bring him his special drink?"

"Well, let's just say I wanted to teach old Hank a lesson," explained TG.

"A lesson," repeated Charlie.

"Yeah," said TG, "I was just getting so tired of telling him to take his special compound with him all the time, like I was some kind of parent or something. Time he learnt to take care of himself. Next time he'll remember to bring his compound."

"If there is a next time," said Charlie, thinking TG had been way harsh.

TG continued with his story as if he hadn't heard Charlie's last comment.

"So this morning, they buried him. I was there, nice little service..." he said thoughtfully.

"Buried him?" gasped Charlie. "But they can't have. He's not dead. We were going to be working on a case together."

"But he *is* dead Charlie," TG interrupted. "At least as far as the police are concerned. It's up to us now. We have to get him out of that box and back into the land of the living. At least until he can solve a case honestly, so that he can face the Court of Ghouls once more."

Charlie shook his head in bewilderment. "And just how do you propose doing that?" he asked. "Going to the graveyard in the dead of night, arming ourselves with spades and digging up the body?"

"My my, Charlie! Ever thought of becoming a detective, kid? That's exactly what we're gonna do!"

Charlie gulped.

"But Hank's okay where he is for the time being," TG continued. "First of all you and I have a case to solve. The details should be with the letter."

Charlie re-opened the envelope and found another

sheet of paper, covered in Hank's untidy scrawl. At the top of the sheet were the words:

THE PRESS REPORTER MURDER

The Grim Reaper stood up and yawned. "I'm going for a nap. Too many late nights catching up with me." He yawned again. "Wake me up before you leave and we can discuss what you've read." TG walked, a little unsteadily, into the bedroom that adjoined Hank Kane's office.

"Okay. Eh …", Charlie wondered what to call The Grim Reaper.

"TG. Just call me TG, kid. Hank always does."

CHAPTER SIX

ON THE CASE

TG LEFT the room and Charlie put the sheet of paper on the desk in front of him. He stood up and got a much needed glass of water. He still felt a bit shaky. This was just too much to take in. Hank was dead, buried somewhere in a grave in Glasgow and he was expected to work hand in hand with The Grim Reaper to solve a murder case!

He sat down again and tried to gather his thoughts. The way he saw it, he had two options. He could leave now, go back home and pretend this whole thing had never happened. Or, he could read the details of the case, try to solve it and dig up Hank's body from the graveyard. He didn't have to think for long. Curiosity killed the cat, his mother always said. Only in this case, Charlie hoped he wouldn't turn out to be the cat! He picked up the sheet of paper and began to read.

Jimmy Casey, a reporter on one of the local newspapers, had been found dead, a few weeks previously, at his Eaglesham home, a village about 2 miles south west of Glasgow. The police who investigated the case said there were no suspicious circumstances. His wife thought differently.

Casey had been carrying out some repairs to the roof of

his house. He had fallen about forty feet from the ladder he was using and had been killed instantly. His wife had been inside working on her computer when she'd heard angry voices outside.

She had hurried outside and was just in time to see a blue car tearing down the driveway at top speed and screech round the corner. Her husband was lying on the ground, dead.

She had given this information to the police but as there were no other witnesses they had made no effort to trace either the blue car, or its driver. Casey's death was recorded as accidental. Pretty sloppy, huh?

Jimmy Casey hadn't done himself any favours in the village and had not been one of its most popular residents. A newcomer to the village, he'd made no friends and made most of his money from other peoples' misfortunes.

He loved dragging up dirt from other peoples' pasts and splashing it all over the front of the newspaper. This made him popular with the editor of the newspaper but one friend and many enemies don't add up to a happy life.

Seems his wife, Anna, wasn't crazy about him either but she wanted to know what was going on. So, she'd called me.

A transcript of the interview between Hank and Anna Casey was there, though this threw up no further clues other than what Charlie already knew.

He wasn't sure where to start. He turned the paper over and saw that Hank had written some clues for him.

"Sorry I can't be of more help to you, kid, but perhaps the following may be of some use."

Below this, in block capital letters, Hank had given Charlie three very obscure clues. They had to be. The Court Of Ghouls had to be convinced that Hank had not solved the case for Charlie.

1. *Go right to the top and take a 'reel' good look at M27.*
2. *Find the right venue and wolf down a sarsaparilla.*
3. *Express yourself, but not to the king, and make sure you're on the right lines, kid.*

Charlie pushed his fingers through his hair. "Reel?" Maybe Hank should learn to spell. He read the clues again but his mind was blank. And no wonder, he'd just had the weirdest morning of his entire life. He couldn't really be expected to think straight!

He put all the papers back in the envelope, tidied Hank's desk and made his way to the door of TG's room. He knocked, gently at first, then more loudly when there was no reply. He was just about to leave when he heard TG grunt, "come in" from inside the room. Charlie pushed the door slightly ajar and put his head just inside.

He swallowed. "I'm on the case TG. Why don't we touch base tomorrow?"

TG pushed himself up from his sleeping position. "Sounds good to me, kid. I'm bushed."

"You seem very cool about Hank being buried alive.

Shouldn't we be doing something about getting him out now?"

TG lay back down and punched his pillows. "Trust me on this one, kid, Hank'll be just fine. He'll have to get used to living with worms and creepy crawlies soon enough, may as well make a start now."

"Another thing, TG. About this office; one minute it's here and the next minute it's gone! What's all that about?"

"Kid, the bottom line is, Hank Kane can only be found when he *wants* to be found. Unless Hank's called you, you won't find this office. And if you show another living soul where it is... well, let's just say you'd regret that."

"But then how did the burglar find it?"

"Good question. But hey, you're the detective – and I'm knackered, you go figure!"

He closed his eyes and immediately went back to sleep.

Charlie left the office, locking the door behind him. He hoped Hank wouldn't be *too* mad when they eventually got around to digging him up!

CHAPTER SEVEN
THE REAPER GOES TO THE MOVIES

When Charlie awoke the next day he was sure the events of the previous day must have been a dream. He stretched, got out of bed and lifted his jacket from where he'd thrown it over the back of his chair. He checked the pocket. Hank's letter was there, with the clues he had to solve. He sat down on the bed and tried to gather his thoughts.

Okay, so it hadn't been a dream. Hank *was* buried somewhere and it was up to him and his new friend, The Grim Reaper, to find him. And solve a murder case. He folded the pieces of paper, put them back in his pocket and went into the bathroom to have a shower. He had a lot of work to do, so he'd better get dressed and get over to Hank's office.

An hour later he knocked on the door of the office and tried not to look shocked when TG opened the door. This guy was going to take a bit of getting used to!

The unlikely pair sat on either side of the desk and spread the sheets of paper out in front of them. They looked at the clues again.

1. *Go right to the top and take a reel good look at M27.*
2. *Find the right venue and wolf down a sarsaparilla.*
3. *Express yourself, but not to the King, and make sure you're on the right lines.*

"Take a 'reel' good look," Charlie said out loud. "A real good look at what?"

TG pointed a skeletal finger at the word "reel". "I don't think that's a spelling mistake, kid. I think Hank's trying to tell you something."

Charlie looked at the clue again.

"But the only kind of reel I know is a reel of film, or maybe a fishing reel?" he looked at TG questioningly.

TG smiled. "Right the first time, kid. Read the clue again."

"Go right to the top… to the top of the cinema!" Charlie said excitedly. "He means the new cinema in town, he must do. It has lots of floors in it, and the seats are numbered. Hank must mean for me to go to the top floor of the cinema and find the right seat number! There must be another clue there for us!"

Charlie was already out of his seat and stuffing the sheets of paper back into his pocket.

"Come on, TG, let's go! We can't hang about here all day."

"Whoa there, calm down," said TG. "We can't go right now, the cinema's not even open yet."

Charlie checked his watch and sat back down, disappointed.

"Oh yeah, right, I'd forgotten how early it was. So when can we go?"

"Tonight," said TG. "We'll go tonight. There's a special showing of *Scream if you Dare* tonight. We'll wait until then and go." He looked down at his clothes. "I think you'll agree it's better if I go out under cover of darkness. If anyone in the cinema wonders about my appearance, I'll say I'm just getting into the atmosphere of the movie! Besides, I have a pretty convincing 'human mask' that I wear for special occasions. I hate to dress down, but needs must!"

Charlie smiled. He had to agree with TG. He certainly wouldn't fancy being one of the audience tonight; being frightened half to death by the film then glancing around to see The Grim Reaper sitting behind you!

They spent the rest of the day putting Hank's office back into some kind of order. When they'd done that, Charlie read every newspaper article he could find on Jimmy Casey's death. There was nothing of any great help so he just had to wait anxiously until it was time to go to the cinema.

Eventually, TG said it was time to go and the two of them set off. The cinema was within walking distance and Charlie noted with some amusement how passers-by gave the twosome a wide berth when they saw them approach.

Though TG had left his huge scythe in the office, he still looked pretty scary, especially when he looked straight at you with his red, burning eyes. Every now and then though, it was TG who was spooked out when he saw "Moshers" or "Goths" - kids who dressed up like they were dead. They looked at TG wondering if he was some sad weirdo trying to relive his youth by dressing like them.

TG had booked the cinema tickets beforehand with one of his credit cards so it was merely a case of picking up their tickets from one of the machines in the foyer. They gave their tickets to one of the cinema staff and though Charlie was under age for the film, he slipped past almost unnoticed. The staff were too busy staring openly at TG, his "human mask" being only partly convincing.

They went inside the darkened cinema and were shown to their seats.

"R7 and R8," whispered Charlie. "We have to find M27 and get the clue."

TG nodded and took his seat. The couple sitting in front glanced round, then turned quickly away, the boy placing his arm protectively around his girlfriend's shoulders. "Weirdo," he mouthed in her ear. The girl smiled back and snuggled into the warmth of her boyfriend's arms. "Weirdo" was an understatement, she thought to herself. And, boy, did he stink!

The film started and the cinema went quiet. Charlie was scared. Though he wouldn't have admitted it for the world, he wasn't a great fan of horror films and would never have come to see this one by choice. He decided to concentrate on working out which seat he and TG had to find. He counted how many rows in front of him row M was and then figured out where seat number 27 was.

He was just about to make his way towards it and find the clue when an extremely overweight man sat down in the seat. The man had already eaten an enormous hot dog and had now started on an extra large bucket of popcorn. His fingers dipped methodically into the bucket, his eyes never leaving the screen.

Charlie glanced at TG. He was completely engrossed in the film and was either smiling or grimacing? Charlie was never quite sure which. He sighed and sat back in his chair. "Looks like we'll have to wait 'till the film's over," he thought. He certainly wasn't even considering asking the man in seat 27 to move! He looked at the screen and willed the film to be over.

One hour and fifteen minutes later, the credits finally began to roll. Charlie's hands were sticky with sweat and his t-shirt clung to him.

"Lot of nonsense," laughed TG as they stretched in their seats. "Can't imagine how anyone would find that scary. I could do much better. Do you think I should get an agent or something, Charlie?"

TG had turned towards Charlie, as if he anticipated an answer. But Charlie was hardly listening as he wiped the beads of sweat from his top lip and tried to smile.

"Not scary?" he thought to himself. He had been terrified out of his wits and would probably have nightmares that night when he went to bed! Still, there was no point in telling that to TG. It wouldn't have done his street cred any good whatsoever!

The cinema was almost empty but Charlie and TG remained seated. Charlie's kept his eyes on the back of the huge guy's head all the time. At last! Charlie thought he'd never get up!

The man edged his way along row M, his enormous bulk making his exit less than easy. Charlie stood up and began making his way forward, with TG following. There were only a few people left in the cinema and they paid little attention to him and the strange looking guy in the black cloak.

Charlie found the seat and knelt down to take a closer look. "Yuck". The guy had put so much mustard on his hot dog that half of it had slopped onto the floor and Charlie had just knelt in it! Between that and crunching through bits of popcorn, Charlie could feel that the knees of his jeans were in a real mess. His mum would be delighted.

He put his hand underneath the seat and felt around. The cinema lights hadn't come back on so it was difficult to see anything. He could feel something, though. Sticky tape, holding what felt like a bit of paper underneath the chair. He put his fingernail under the tape and pulled so he could release the piece of paper.

"Got it," he told TG triumphantly. "Let's go. We won't be able to read it in here."

The two of them left the cinema and made their

way down the escalators to the outer doors of the
cinema. It was dark outside and they walked quickly
towards the light of a street lamp. Charlie unfolded
the piece of paper and both of them read what was
written there.

It was a car registration number.

CHAPTER EIGHT

MRS CASEY

CHARLIE knocked on the front door of the large house. He'd tried ringing the doorbell but it became clear that it was out of order. However, Anna Casey didn't keep him waiting long after his first knock. She opened the door, smiled briefly and invited Charlie in, apologising for the fact that the doorbell wasn't working.

"My Jimmy – God bless him – he was no handyman," she said.

Charlie had telephoned earlier that morning, told Mrs Casey who he was and asked if he could call on her. Though Hank's client was a bit put out that Hank himself wasn't calling on her to give an update, she had accepted Charlie's explanation of Hank suddenly being called away on other urgent business. Charlie had also assured her that Hank would be back on the case just as soon as he returned and no doubt would be calling on her in the future.

Charlie sat down in the spacious lounge and took his notebook from his pocket. Anna Casey sat opposite and looked at him, for the first time realising just how young this "detective" was. Charlie sensed she was becoming more dubious by the second, due to his obvious youth.

"I know, I know, I look young for my age," he said.

"What age are you, then?"

"Old enough to be trusted by Hank Kane," said Charlie, deciding to try and act like Hank. "Lady, d'ya think I'd be here if I couldn't handle things? The minute I let you down, you can drop me from the case. What d'ya say, fair deal?"

Intrigued by this young man's obvious confidence, Anna Casey put her doubts aside for the moment.

"I suppose so."

Charlie could hardly believe his act was working. He cleared his throat.

"Okay," he said, as he flicked through his notebook. "It says here in Hank's notes that you saw a car leaving your driveway pretty quickly on the morning of the, eh, accident?"

"There was no accident. If by 'accident' you mean 'murder', then the car in question was a blue one. Don't ask me what make it was."

"Okay. It would be very helpful if you could remember even a few of the numbers on the registration plate."

Mrs Casey took a scrap of paper from the pocket of her jeans.

"I did, actually. I managed to catch the first three digits, not that those numbskulls from the forces of law and order were interested. Said they couldn't hope to match them to anything."

She read out, 'X67', "something, something,

something. I couldn't see the rest, the car was going too fast."

Charlie glanced down at the registration number he had written in his notebook. X679 XSG.

He didn't want to give too much away. "We *may* have something, Mrs Casey, but I'd like to get back to the office and check a few things before I say any more. By the way, can you think of a reason why someone would want to kill Jimmy? Was he rich, had he offended anyone, or what?"

"Well, I'm sure when you investigate his bank statements, you'll see a deposit for £50,000, from the newspaper he worked for, *The Globe*. It was an advance to encourage him to complete some big report. Don't ask me what it was about. It's no secret that Jimmy and I didn't take much interest in each other's lives."

Anna Casey showed Charlie out. "You will keep in touch, won't you? And ask your boss to give me a call when he gets back, please."

Charlie said that he would 'keep her informed of all developments as the case progressed'. He impressed himself with his grasp of detective jargon but wondered if Anna Casey realised just how impossible her last request might be.

£50,000! Wow, thought Charlie, the editor of *The Globe* must have really wanted that story!

CHAPTER NINE

ON THE TOWN WITH TG

BACK at Hank's office, Charlie was puzzling over Hank's second clue.

2. *Find the right venue and wolf down a sarsaparilla.*

Charlie pushed a handful of crisps into his mouth and munched thoughtfully. Sarsaparilla wasn't something he was used to drinking and just how was he supposed to find the right venue? How would he even *know* he'd found the right venue? He sighed and began to doodle on the page.

TG joined him from the other room.

"Hey, TG. Thought you'd never surface this morning."

Charlie had learned since he'd got to know The Grim Reaper that the guy liked to party on down all night and sleep late all day, or most of it. Charlie didn't know where he spent all his nights but he sure looked like he had a good time!

TG took a large gulp of his coffee and sat down. "Didn't get to bed till real late, kid. This town is such a fun place to be!"

Charlie didn't doubt TG's word, but for now his priority was solving clues two and three and rescuing Hank.

"Any ideas on this one, TG?" he pointed to the clue with his pencil.

TG smiled. "Sure do, kid. In fact I can take you there, though I think it would be fair to say you should prepare yourself for a bit of a shock!"

"You can take me there?" exclaimed Charlie. "But that's brilliant! When can we go? Can we go now?"

TG was becoming used to the kid's impatience. "Tonight, Charlie. The joint doesn't open till late. Go home, chill out, do something kids do for a change. Come back when it's dark."

"Something kids do?" Charlie was offended. "I'm not a kid, TG, and the sooner you and Hank realise that, the better."

He took his notebook and pencil, lifted his jacket and left the office. TG took another sip of coffee and decided to go back to bed.

*   *   *   *   *   *   *

It was almost ten o'clock when Charlie and TG approached a cash machine next to a derelict building. They waited for a customer to finish his transaction. As the customer moved away, TG walked forward and keyed a secret code into the machine.

"Stand right there," said TG pointing to a spot in front of the building, "and when you get to the other side, wait. Don't worry, I'll be right behind you."

Charlie did as he was told. Everything was so weird

these days, he had decided it was easier not to question the instructions he was given.

In a few seconds a door to the derelict building opened. Charlie went through the doorway and found himself inside a musty corridor somewhere behind the cash machine.

He dusted himself down, having picked up some cobwebs on the way, and waited for TG. He didn't have long to wait.

"This way, kid, follow me," urged TG, who looked very animated and happy. Almost as though he had come to life. He walked ahead of Charlie, taking huge, long strides. Charlie had great difficulty keeping up with him. The corridor was long and very, dark. Hundreds of cobwebs draped from the ceiling and it smelt of something that Charlie couldn't quite identify. He stopped, briefly, to brush a particularly thick cobweb off his jacket but when he looked up, TG had disappeared.

Charlie quickened his pace. TG couldn't be *that* far in front he told himself. He decided that he didn't much like being here. He rounded a corner. Surely he'd see TG now? But there was only another long, dark, empty corridor.

Charlie kept walking. He couldn't help thinking how weird it was that he was desperately trying to catch up with none other than The Grim Reaper. There was something not quite right about that but at the moment he had no option. He had to find TG.

He came to a door halfway down the corridor. There was no sign on the outside, nothing to tell him what lay behind it, but he decided to push it open anyway.

The heavy door creaked and groaned as it opened. He had just known it would. "TG," he called out, though his voice sounded weak and hollow to his ears. He cleared his throat noisily and tried again.

"TG?" he called, louder this time. "Are you in here?"

There was total silence. Then, from somewhere in the far corner came a scuttling noise. Oh no, thought Charlie. Not spiders, please, not spiders.

His eyes had grown accustomed to the dark and he was able to make out that a heavy, velvet curtain was dividing the room in two. It hung from the centre of the ceiling and it was from behind the curtain that the scuttling noise came from.

Charlie's sister, Annie, had explained to him many times that it was very unlikely that you'd ever actually *hear* spiders, unless they were the type that wore big heavy boots with steel toe-caps. So Charlie tried to think straight. He comforted himself with the thought that the scuttling was probably just rats, or ghosts, or monsters – anything except spiders!

Charlie knew he should leave. It was pretty obvious TG wasn't in the room; he *knew* he could hear spiders and he was more than a little scared. Still, there was something about that velvet curtain which made him want to take a tiny, little peek. He knew he'd never rest unless he saw what was behind it.

He started to move forward gingerly, trying to watch where he placed his feet. He had no desire to step on a spider and hear it crunch beneath his trainers. That smell assailed his nostrils, again. It smelled like something that had been dead for a long time. Rotting flesh. The way TG smelt. Maybe he *was* in the room after all!

Charlie reached out and touched the curtain. The scuttling noises had become louder, more frantic. In fact, he wasn't even sure it *was* scuttling he was hearing. It sounded more like something was being *devoured* in there. He took a deep breath and pulled back the curtain.

When he saw what lay before him, he wished he'd never touched the curtain.

CHAPTER TEN
THE CESSPIT

A BADLY decomposed body was spread out on a table. Charlie could hardly see the body because it was almost covered in small, black creatures. They seemed to be some kind of spider. Their legs thrashed about as they fought one another for any part of the body, that still had some flesh attached to it.

The sucking, grinding noises they were making was awful. They were literally *gorging* themselves. There was no other word for it. Gorging themselves on the flesh of some poor, dead guy. If it was a guy; the body was barely recognisable even as a human being.

Charlie felt himself beginning to throw up. He put his hand over his mouth and tried to steady himself. He put his other hand against the wall and immediately pulled it away. The wall was damp and slimy and Charlie's hands felt sticky and wet. Shaking, he fell against the curtain and made his way back to the door. There was nothing he could do for the poor guy on the table; he had to get himself out of the room, and fast.

He reached the heavy door and pulled the handle. The door wouldn't move. He began to throw up. He just couldn't help it. He pulled the handle harder but his hands kept slipping from the wet substance the wall had coated them in. Eventually the door began to open, and Charlie almost threw himself outside.

Gasping with relief, he sank to the floor. He looked at his hands, more visible now in the slightly better lit corridor.

"Oh no!" he cried, recoiling in horror. The substance on his hands was blood. He had someone's blood on his hands. Frantically he tried to wipe the stickiness on the floor. Like someone demented he wiped again and again, each time re-examining his hands, hoping to see them looking clean again. Whose blood was it, he wondered? Where had TG brought him to? What terrible place was this?

Charlie stood, leaning against the wall for support. Then feeling a bit better, he tried to stand on his own two feet in the corridor. He had no idea what direction he should take. He had completely lost his bearings now and didn't know whether the room he had just come from had been on his right or left hand side.

"Charlie?"

He heard his name being called from somewhere in the distance. It was TG.

"I never would have thought I'd be glad to see The Grim Reaper," thought Charlie, "but at last he's come back to find me.

"I'm here!" shouted Charlie, trying to keep his voice from shaking.

TG seemed to materialise from the darkness.

"I thought I'd lost you, kid. Quit your messing and

try and keep up. Come on, let's go. The nightclub's straight ahead."

Charlie decided to ignore TG's comment about "messing". He'd say nothing about his latest adventure for the moment. He chose instead to keep silent and follow TG, very closely.

Just up ahead, Charlie could see a sign above a doorway. He shook his head in disbelief. The sign read: "The Cesspit".

It was the entrance to a nightclub.

The bouncers were monsters. Literally. Scaly, slimy creatures with loose flesh hanging from their faces and blood running from the corners of their mouths. Charlie was repulsed and moved inside quickly.

"It's a bank holiday for the Court of Ghouls and I recommended Glasgow as a place for a staff night out. Even monsters need to have fun! Do you think the tourist board would pay me a commission for introducing such fine customers to their city?"

"Wha...wha...what *are* they?" asked Charlie, barely able to believe his own eyes.

"Human, believe it or not. Yes, I know, hardly what you'd call human. But you've got to remember, the folks at the Court of Ghouls have been dead for hundreds of years. Problem is, they don't go to heaven or hell, they stay forever in this twilight zone between life and death."

"You mean like Hank?" asked Charlie, who was just still very wary.

"Yeah, but at least in Hank's case it's temporary. He can 'move on', as we say, once the Court decides that he has solved a case honestly, without cheating. These guys just continue to decompose! And every day, something new, something ugly decides to grow on the remains of their flesh, bacteria mostly. You know, these guys are like walking laboratories. I mean, creatures have practically evolved on these guys! That's why they look so…"

"Gross?" ventured Charlie.

"… different, I was going to say. But hey, if 'gross' is more like it, Charlie, then *you* can tell 'em that."

"Different, you say? I think 'different' sounds a lot better, TG."

Everywhere Charlie looked the sights that greeted him were mind blowing. Every creature imaginable (and some unimaginable) seemed to congregate here. He never thought he'd say it but he was actually glad of TG's company!

He followed TG to the bar where they ordered drinks. Charlie looked along the shelves and was surprised to see the only drink on sale seemed to be sarsaparilla! Rows and rows of the pink liquid glistened against the dark wood of the bar.

A small fridge housed bottles of alcopop, bearing the name 'Alcosparilla', the beer barrel read 'Beersparilla'. It appeared that sarsaparilla was the only liquid that dead people could drink!

Charlie sucked on his straw and looked around the

bar. Some creatures looked familiar. Vampires, Frankenstein-type monsters and, of course a few ghosts all joined the Court of Ghouls staff as they danced, drank, shouted, and screamed their way through the night.

Suddenly Charlie became aware of a hand being placed on his arm. It was a very large, hairy hand, which had claws instead of nails. The claws dug into his shoulder and he could feel his flesh being bruised. He turned around. He could only describe the thing that touched him as an animal. He resembled a wolf, his face and body completely covered in hair, his teeth sharpened and glistening beneath a snout. Charlie tried to free himself of the animal's grip, but its hold was firm.

"Hey, Wolfy! Howya doin'?" said TG, as they gave each other "five."

Charlie felt the grip loosen from his shoulder and the animal seemed to relax somewhat. Its breath was warm on Charlie's face when he spoke.

"Okay, TG, doin' okay," growled the wolf-like figure.

Charlie looked from one to the other.

"Is this the kid Hank was going on about?" he grunted heavily.

TG nodded. "This is Charlie, he's sort of new to all this, but I've brought him here because we really need your help."

As though a fog had cleared, Charlie suddenly remembered the words of clue number two.

2. *Find the right venue and wolf down a sarsaparilla.*

He was in the right venue, had met a werewolf and was drinking sarsaparilla!

"And I'm always glad to be of assistance," growled the werewolf, pulling his claws through Charlie's hair as he spoke.

Charlie tried not to flinch. Sensing his discomfort, TG spoke. "We're in a bit of a rush tonight, Hank's in trouble, so if you can give us the information?"

"Like I care about Hank Kane. So he's in trouble tonight. Big deal. When's that guy not in trouble? Pretty hard to stay out of trouble when all he does is go looking for it."

TG picked the werewolf up by the throat and pushed him against the wall. Charlie was seeing TG at his worst. Now he really appreciated having him on his side.

"Now you listen to me, Weird Wolf. I know a few guys roaming this city with silver bullets loaded and ready to fire into your mangy fur. Maybe I should point them in your direction, huh? I got enough money put aside to pay any number of bounty hunters. Besides, think of the money I could make when the headline, 'Werewolf Found Mangled In Dark Glasgow Alley' hits the streets. What a story – and you know I got contacts at the *Examiner*, and the *Globe*. So….you can help, yeah?"

"I see Hank Kane's brutal policing methods are rubbing off on you, TG," moaned Wolfy.

He drained his glass and handed it to Charlie. Charlie noticed it had a piece of paper stuck to it.

"Be my guest," he snarled through clenched teeth. "Maybe we'll meet again, Kid, under a full moon perhaps?"

"Not if I see you first, Weirdo Wolf," said Charlie tearing the piece of paper off the glass. Having The Grim Reaper beside him encouraged such bravery.

He and TG left the nightclub; TG somewhat reluctantly as the resident DJ had just taken over the decks and TG could feel his party head reappearing. Still, there was work to be done, and he led the way down the corridor and outside.

"Remind me to keep an eye on you at the next full moon!" said TG, smiling at Charlie. He'd been impressed with his courage.

"You mean in case the werewolf gets me?" laughed Charlie with mounting bravado.

"No, in case you get him!"

Charlie breathed a huge sigh of relief on getting back to the centre of town. The bravado was false. It masked his fear. Not that TG was fooled. After all, fear was something The Grim Reaper was an expert in.

Charlie examined the piece of paper which he'd removed from the glass. It was a receipt for a painting called:

Catch Me If You Can, by Goe N. Togetya
Sold To: Mr James Casey

On the other side of the receipt was written:

Mortimer's ~ Art Dealers, Sauchiehall St, Glasgow
Director ~ Arthur J Mortimer

"So, our Jimmy bought a painting? Goe N. Togetya? Famous Hungarian painter, I believe. 19th Century. Is there a date on the receipt, kid?"
Charlie looked more closely at the receipt.
"Yep, a week before he died. Look TG…" began Charlie. "If you want to go back inside, don't let me stop you. I'm heading off home now, anyway."
TG tried to look reluctant, but failed miserably. He knew Charlie was determined to prove to Hank and himself that he wasn't just a kid; that he could do the job and was as brave as they come.
TG also knew that his sixth sense was so well developed that he could practically follow the kid in his mind, wherever he was. Thanks to his psychic powers he could be with Charlie in an instant should any danger threaten him. He didn't tell Charlie this though. Why not let the kid feel like he was in control?
"Well, if you're sure, I mean I can come with you to the bus stop…"
"Really TG, feel free. I'm just glad to have found the second clue. You go on. I'll talk to you tomorrow."
TG nodded. "Okay kid, if you're sure you're okay. I'll see you tomorrow. Not too early, though." He

went off to party but with his mind's eye on Charlie.

Charlie smiled and walked towards his bus stop. If hanging out with the living dead in The Cesspit nightclub was what TG was into, he was welcome to it. But then, Charlie wondered, what would amuse *him* if *he* were the messenger of death?

CHAPTER ELEVEN

CATCH ME IF YOU CAN

MORTIMER'S, the Art Dealers, was situated in one of the more up-market areas of town. Charlie smiled to himself as he realised the initials of 'Mortimer's the Art Dealers' spelt, 'MAD'.

As he pushed open the door, a bell rang loudly above him. A sharp featured man was crouched down beside the desk, rummaging about in a box, as if he'd lost something. Charlie's entrance seemed to annoy him and he barely looked up from what he was doing.

"Yes? May I be of some assistance, *sir*?" he asked as he looked at Charlie, sourly. The word 'sir' sounded like it had been forced out of him.

Charlie drew himself up to his full height of five feet nothing.

"I was admiring a painting in your window, the one with the sunset scene. The style reminds me of another painting, the name of which escapes me right now. There's no price tag, perhaps you can tell me how much it costs?"

The man sniffed and went over to look at the painting in the window. "None of our paintings carry price tags. What sort of price range are you considering, *sir*? This time, the man was almost spitting the word 'sir'.

"Well, price isn't that important really," replied Charlie, ignoring the man's contempt. "I really just wanted to find a similar painting to the sunset one you have in your window. You see, style's my thing – not cost."

Charlie felt really proud of his speech. What utter rubbish he was talking! He had exactly £15.76 in his pocket, but the haughty man in front of him wasn't to know that!

The man reluctantly looked up a stock sheet and checked the price of the painting.

"The sunset painting is £7,500," he said, "without the frame."

Charlie gulped, then quickly tried to recover.

"Maybe I should speak to your boss about that price. I know I said the price isn't the most important thing here, but that doesn't mean I want to get ripped off."

"I *am* the boss," said the man, as he struggled to remain calm.

"You're Mortimer?"

"*Mr* Mortimer, *sir*."

"Fine. I'll need a couple of days to think about it. "Oh, I've just remembered the name of that similar painting. It was called, *'Catch Me If You Can'* – do you remember that one? I saw it in your shop a few weeks ago?"

The man turned white, gulped then just as quickly recovered his composure.

"I don't remember it, sir. I'm sorry. I'm sure you'll

understand, we have such a lot of transactions every week."

Charlie nodded, although the man's reaction hadn't gone unnoticed. A box of frames lay to Charlie's left and he subconsciously fingered them as he spoke.

"Was sir interested in purchasing a frame?" asked Mortimer.

Charlie glanced down at the box. "No, not really, though perhaps I will need one for the painting I intend buying." The only thing Charlie was really buying was time, instinctively knowing that the trick in detective work was to hang in there, even when there seemed to be no point. How else would you ever come across the unexpected?

He lifted a frame from the box. There was a scrap of paper attached to it. Then he remembered that this was the box the guy was rummaging in, just as he'd come in. He gingerly slotted the paper between his fingers and slipped it into his pocket. The frame he was holding was made of dark wood, the bottom part of the frame had two parallel lines, one of silver and one of gold.

"Very distinctive," Charlie remarked, somehow sounding like an expert.

"They're made on the premises," sniffed the owner. "Can't buy them anywhere else, they're exclusive to Mortimer's."

Charlie however was only pretending to listen. He was actually looking at what appeared to be an A4 print of a painting. It wasn't the painting that had caught his attention though, it was the title of it, which stood out in big, bold letters:

Catch Me If You Can

Strange then that Mortimer didn't even recognise the title when Charlie had said it, considering a print of it was practically staring him in the face at the time!

Charlie nodded and put the frame back in the box. "Thanks for your help," he said, "I'll be back."

He left the shop, the door clanging shut behind him. So, what did Charlie have to go on? Not a lot. Just a hunch, that Mortimer was not just hiding something but was up to his neck in something very dodgy.

What proof do I have? thought Charlie. None. Do I have anything to link Mortimer to Casey? Apart from the receipt given to me so graciously by Weirdo Wolf? Well, he thought, I'll keep that card up my sleeve for the moment. No point in letting Mortimer know I'm on to him. Plus, explaining where I got it from, to the police, might be just a tad tricky!

There was also Anna Casey's memory of part of the car registration. But while Charlie had been able to use that, together with the clue relating to the cinema, it was not a definitive match. Charlie knew he now needed to work on clue number three.

CHAPTER TWELVE

TRAIN TO NOWHERE

CHARLIE had found that the third clue had been the easiest towork out.

3. *Express yourself, but not to the king, and make sure you're on the right lines.*

He had known that Express trains ran regularly from Glasgow Queen Street to Waverley Station in Edinburgh. TG had bought tickets for the 4am to Edinburgh after Charlie had reported to him what had happened at Mortimer's. Charlie hadn't known there was a train so early but TG had assured him there was.

TG and Charlie waited on the platform at Queen St Station. TG had made an effort to look a little less conspicuous. He'd not only put on his human mask, but also the new suit he'd "acquired" from a recently dead soul he'd collected for the Court Of Ghouls. Charlie had looked disapprovingly at TG when he'd told him how he'd come across the suit.

"What! Oh c'mon kid, it's not like the guy needed it. Let me tell you, where he's going, all this smart material would have got badly singed for sure! What a waste. One other thing, Charlie," TG added, as he stood admiring his reflection in the window of a passing train, "I may have forgotten to explain that the train we're getting is, how shall I put this? A special train."

"What do you mean?" asked Charlie, beginning to feel somewhat anxious.

"Eh, some of my friends might be on this train."

"Oh, brilliant, absolutely brilliant! Just what I need at this time of the morning, a nightmare, a waking nightmare. Your friends from the other night I presume? Ever heard the expression 'with friends like that you don't need enemies'? So what's this then – The Ghost Train?"

"You're sounding more like Hank every day, kid."

"Thanks."

"It wasn't a compliment."

"Don't worry, none taken."

The "special" train pulled alongside their platform and the pair of them boarded.

Charlie sat down on the first seat he came to and TG sat down next to him. He looked out of the window, his mind working away furiously. How was Hank holding up? Would he be the same? Might he need to take a back seat in future investigations and let "the kid" take over the front line investigation work? Could this be the chance Charlie had been waiting for all his life? Only if he solved this case, he thought.

A conductor came round to check their tickets. A conductor, the likes of whom Charlie had never seen before! If Charlie spent all his remaining days in Hell, he hoped the devil himself wouldn't look like the dripping, foul smelling creature who now put out his hand to take Charlie's ticket.

This *thing* was red in colour, had horns on its head and black hooves as feet. His eyes devoured Charlie, taking in every aspect, and Charlie felt as if he were being pulled towards him.

Charlie tried to look away, tried to resist, but the force of the creature was too strong. He felt his hand lift from the arm-rest of his chair and reach out.

TG did nothing to stop the kid's movement and Charlie leaned further forward in his seat. The horned devil for, indeed, that was what he was, placed his burning hand in Charlie's and held it there for what seemed like an eternity.

"Your ticket, kid, your ticket," said TG, "even on a ghost train you need a ticket."

"I thought you had the tickets, TG," whispered Charlie.

"Oh yeah, hold on." TG searched his pockets for a while and then gave up. He looked at the inspector sheepishly, adding, "You'll never believe me but, I think I left them in my other suit. Anyway, don't you owe me a few favours? Like how's that cream I gave you for the horns. They've grown back I see." The inspector shrugged and shuffled from hoof to hoof.

TG glanced at Charlie saying, "Don't ask. Long story; involves a cheeky devil, a mallet and an impatient Grim Reaper." He looked back at the inspector. "I think you have something for the kid."

Again, Charlie's hand was taken but this time something was placed in it. A piece of soft shiny card.

Reluctantly, the creature moved on, looking further down the carriages of the train for other innocent souls who might lurk there. Charlie could hear him muttering to himself, "*Everyone* owes you favours, TG."

The train drew to a halt and TG told Charlie it was time to get off. Charlie was amazed to see that they were back in Glasgow, Queen Street, at the exact same place where they had boarded the ghostly (or was that ghastly?) train.

He looked down at the card that the inspector had placed in his hand. It was a photograph. A photograph of a painting. A painting Charlie had seen a print of. It was the one Jimmy Casey had bought: *Catch Me If You Can*.

And the wooden frame which surrounded the picture had the familiar silver and gold lines which Charlie recognised from his visit to Mortimer's shop.

CHAPTER THIRTEEN

CASE CLOSED?

ARTHUR Mortimer was indignant when he was arrested. "I know nothing about a Jimmy Casey," he protested as the police placed handcuffs on his wrists and escorted him from the shop. "You've got the wrong man, I tell you, why won't anyone listen to me?"

Charlie's job was done, and it was now up to the police to deal with it. He had been able to check that the car registration number was indeed Mortimer's car. He had handed in his notes to the police and they had taken over.

Arthur Mortimer, according to the official police version, had met Jimmy Casey in the very recent past. Jimmy had turned up a story on Mortimer, which would have made for an extremely embarrassing headline.

Casey was no art lover. He'd turned up at Mortimer's and bought the first painting he'd seen, *Catch Me If You Can*, to explain his presence there. Then he'd sniffed out some of the information he'd needed for his story.

Casey only had part of the story but he had enough to know that Mortimer, Glasgow's most important Art Dealer, was in deep trouble and was terrified that his wife would find out.

Mrs Mortimer came from a very wealthy family but her husband and his gallery had been in financial trouble for years. If his wife and her powerful family found out they would probably cut him off without a penny.

Of course, Casey being Casey, he couldn't resist the temptation of blackmailing Mortimer. It was the nature of the man.

Mortimer knew even the hint of a scandal would ruin him. He'd gone to Casey's home to try and plead with him not to expose him in the newspaper. Unfortunately, Mortimer had become so angry that he'd shaken the ladder Casey was on and made him fall. He hadn't *meant* to kill him.

Mortimer realised straight away that Casey was dead. After a moment of panic, he realised he'd actually got lucky. Then he got even luckier. After Casey had fallen, Mortimer was running back to his own car when he noticed the painting, *Catch Me If You Can*, lying on the back seat of Casey's car, still in its cellophane wrapping. Luckier still, the car was unlocked.

Acting on a desperate impulse, Mortimer opened the door and grabbed the painting. He didn't want anyone having any reason to link him to the crime. Ironic then that by wasting precious getaway time grabbing the painting from Casey's car, Mortimer had given Mrs Casey the chance to see his car and get half the registration number.

The shame and stress of recent events proved too much for Mortimer. His wife didn't know exactly what he'd been up to but knew it was something that would probably bring embarrassment to the family. She refused to stand by him.

It was obvious that Mortimer's the Art Dealers, would go out of business in a matter of days. The owner's reputation was destroyed, probably more by going bust than by being linked with a murder case. Mortimer died of a heart attack in Baird Street Police Station, hours after being arrested, taking his secrets with him.

CHAPTER FOURTEEN
TEA WITH MRS CASEY

CHARLIE once again found himself in Anna Casey's home, this time feeling even less comfortable than before.

"I must confess to owing you an apology, Mr Christian," said Mrs Casey as she poured Charlie a cup of tea. "I really wasn't sure you were up to the job. But you proved me wrong."

"I proved a lot of things, Mrs Casey, not all of which I shared with the police," replied Charlie.

"What more is there to prove? Mortimer killed my husband. And my 'lovely' husband was blackmailing him…"

"Yes," interrupted Charlie, "but what for?"

"Well, Mr Christian, it appears we'll never know… Mortimer has taken that information to his grave."

"Sorry Mrs Casey. But we both know, don't we?"

"I've lost you completely. What are you talking about?"

"Your husband, Jimmy Casey was on to something wasn't he? A big scoop. What I'm wondering is, where he got the idea that Glasgow's famous Art Dealer, was up to no good."

"Journalists snoop around famous people all the time. It's what they do best. It's certainly what Jimmy did best."

"But all the better. *So much* the better if his *wife* was in a position to give him a hot lead. And if the story becomes big, Jimmy, might just make a lot of money. It's nice to be married to money, Mrs Casey, isn't it? It means it all becomes yours if anything tragic happens to your husband."

"I have no idea what you're talking about. And what would I know about being rich? Jimmy was never what you'd call rich. That £50,000 made up for two years of debt."

"But if that story had come out... Mrs Casey, let's put our cards on the table. Mortimer was being blackmailed because many of the paintings he sold in his gallery were stolen. Stolen from little old ladies, who mysteriously died of old age— "

"There's nothing 'mysterious' about dying of old age— "

"But that's not the mysterious bit. They all had left valuable works of art in their wills to someone who'd recently befriended them. And, what a coincidence that they all passed away soon afterwards."

"Well that's not nice at all," said Mrs Casey, pouring more tea into Charlie's cup, before adding, "not nice but not stealing either, though."

"But Mrs Casey," pointed out Charlie, "They were the lucky ones. Other folks, ones that didn't make a new will benefiting their new friend, met with nasty accidents. The one thing they all had in common is that they all died after coming into contact with a new art-loving friend. A killer is what we are dealing with here."

"Well, I gathered that, silly. Mortimer is...sorry... *was* the killer," said Mrs Casey.

"Not one with a lot of experience, Mrs Casey. Not one who carefully thought out every move. No, Mortimer was too temperamental. He killed Jimmy accidentally remember? What we're dealing with here is a cold-blooded, cold-hearted killer."

"How dreadful. Really terrible," said Mrs Casey, deeply concerned. "But who on earth would ever do such horrible things?"

"You would," said Charlie.

CHAPTER FIFTEEN

ON THE ROPES

CHARLIE had never heard a pin drop before but it was certainly quiet enough to hear one drop now. Mrs Casey looked like she was desperately trying to think of a good lie. Charlie knew he had her off balance so he continued,

"You always wanted more out of life than poor old Jimmy could offer. People thought Jimmy was the nosiest reporter in town but it was you who pushed Jimmy to snoop around. You always thought he'd find something out about the people he investigated – something they'd pay a lot of money to cover up."

Mrs Casey spluttered and gasped, too flabbergasted to actually say anything. Charlie went on,

"You usually kicked things off by doing a tiny bit of investigating of your own. And you'd normally find something pretty scandalous. You discovered Mortimer's secret was that his Gallery was not making money. Not a crime – but not something he wanted to broadcast!

"You're no art lover either, Mrs Casey. The only reason you befriended little old ladies, or anyone else who owned valuable paintings, was to get your hands on their art – which you persuaded Mortimer to buy from you for his gallery.

"Of course, you were sensible enough to use a false

name from the start. At first he couldn't believe his luck! His art gallery was going bust and you just happened to turn up with valuable paintings. He was too desperate to question where you got them. He just knew he could sell them for great prices. He didn't even question why you wanted so little for them!"

"You're wrong, Mr Christian, so wrong," spluttered Mrs Casey. But she had trouble breathing now, never mind speaking and Charlie knew he had her on the ropes, so he kept going.

"You had no idea how much money you could have gotten for them. So when you realised he was not just saving his business but now making a healthy profit too, you felt cheated. Mrs Casey, you were cheated – by your own ignorance of art. So you told Mortimer how you really came to possess such fine paintings and he was shocked. And then you told him that if he didn't pay you a share of his excellent profits, then you'd tell the police that he was dealing in stolen goods. But he was no fool. He'd tell them who the thief was – you! So you had no chance of getting him to pay you a penny."

Mrs Casey, although she could barely speak, looked like she hadn't yet given up on the notion of protesting. So Charlie kept going.

"I never imagined the perfect crime could actually be committed. *You're* the one that proved *me* wrong. It was *you* who told your husband, Jimmy, that there was a story to be had at the Art Gallery, something about 'dodgy gear'. You told him just enough to excite his interest. You knew he'd go snooping and you knew Mortimer would pay this reporter to shut his mouth, or risk going to jail. Not only that, but he had a heart condition that made sure he wanted as little stress and fuss as possible.

"And guess what – it all goes to plan. So Mortimer is paying Jimmy not to tell what he knows. But Mrs Casey, Jimmy didn't know the whole thing was set-up by his own wife! You make money from selling Mortimer the stolen paintings then your husband blackmails him for receiving stolen goods! Whatever money Jimmy was able to squeeze out of Mortimer would end up with you – you were his wife after all. And all the time the only person who knows what's really going on is you! Beautiful, Mrs Casey, Absolutely beautiful. You couldn't make it up."

"You just have! What nonsense! Why would I give my husband a lead that might help him discover I was an art thief – which I wasn't?"

"Because if your *husband* was the investigator, he'd confide in you as to what he'd discovered! And this way, you could monitor the whole investigation. You'd know how much Mortimer was paying, when and where. So you knew that Mortimer was paying Jimmy suitcases full of cash in blackmail money over the months. And if Jimmy ever started to guess too much, you'd know how to cover your tracks, or at least guide him off the trail. So, I'd say you had the 'getting caught' angle covered, wouldn't you?"

"Look, I know my husband wasn't the best of men but I loved him. And even if I didn't, that doesn't mean I'd want him killed. And besides, even the police say the murder was an accident of sorts."

"Mrs Casey, if I had to bet on anyone being able to plan an accident, my money would be on you every time, " said Charlie.

"Let's just say for a moment you're right – which you're not. Then just how could anyone plan on Mortimer shaking the ladders, which by a big coincidence, had my husband on them at the time?"

Charlie paused. He wanted to choose his words carefully.

"Mrs Casey. People say detectives are cynical. Well the first thing we lose faith in is 'coincidence'. Very little happens that is not planned in someway. We work on the basis that there is no coincidence. Your husband had the reputation of a bully. My enquiries suggest that your husband was a scallywag– not a bully. And, you knew Mortimer had a bit of a temper. You counted on him becoming angry when you told him that 'some reporter' had been asking you questions about Mortimer, and that you thought this reporter was onto you both. The phone records for the pay phone down the street show that you called Mortimer's Gallery just before he turned up here in a predictable rage. Of course, he had no idea you were Jimmy's wife, or that you lived here. But then you were conveniently out of sight weren't you?"

Charlie paused again. But Mrs Casey's silence just kept inviting him to continue.

"Jimmy meanwhile was way up the ladder. You said yourself that Jimmy was no handyman, Mrs Casey. So what was he doing up there? He wouldn't have noticed saw-marks on the ladder, would he? He barely knew what a saw looked like. But you did. You'd used one to partly cut the ladder. Then you'd waited until Jimmy was actually up the ladder.

"Mrs Casey, you nagged him to fix the roof. Even if it had needed fixing, it could have waited until the next day, when you could have called a proper tradesman. But *you* couldn't wait because you knew Mortimer was on his way round, didn't you? You knew Jimmy was no fighter, you knew he'd stay on the ladder. And you knew Mortimer would probably shake the ladder, which would break thanks to your handy work with the saw!"

CHAPTER SIXTEEN

POOR MRS CASEY

AFTER a long pause Charlie started to speak but Mrs Casey put her hand up in a gesture that told him not to. Then she began to speak slowly and clearly.

"Have you ever been poor, Mr Christian?"

"I'm poor now!"

Mrs Casey looked up, as if a lifeline had been thrown to her.

"You don't have to be," she said, "Mr Christian... Charlie..."

"It's all over, Mrs Casey," Charlie said in his best Humphrey Bogart style.

Mrs Casey suddenly realised that it was no use.

"Where did I go wrong, Charlie, where did I go wrong?"

Charlie needed to state it all thoroughly and clearly. How else could he be sure that he'd got it one hundred per cent right? He took a deep breath and then began to explain.

"When you sold the first painting, *Catch Me If You Can*, to Mortimer, he'd insisted on a receipt for the money he'd paid you right there and then. In fact, he would not even take the painting from you until you did so. You didn't want him to become suspicious so you bought a receipt book from a nearby stationer and handwrote it in the store. Later, when Mortimer got less fussy and more greedy, he stopped pushing you for receipts.

And it didn't bother you that he still had that receipt somewhere because you'd signed a false name and address. In fact you hoped Jimmy *would* find it as he was losing interest in his investigation. He needed a lead to encourage him to keep going, if he was to start blackmailing Mortimer – and you were counting on the cash from the blackmail.

"The day I visited the gallery, and pretended to look at picture frames, I found the receipt you'd hastily written to Mortimer's for *Catch Me If You Can*, the day you sold it to the gallery. It had clearly come from a small invoice pad stocked by *The Book Store*, where I'd recently bought my stationary for school."

"How could you know that?" snapped Mrs Casey.

"Because that invoice pad is *The Book Store's* own value brand, with their own logo all over it. My kid sister could've worked that one out, Mrs Casey. And as I'd already come across a Mortimer's receipt for *Catch Me If You Can*, issued *by* Mortimer's when *they'd* sold it on, I was curious, to say the least."

"So how did that lead you to me? I'd used a false name remember," wondered Mrs Casey aloud.

"I went to *The Book Store* and asked if anyone remembered selling an invoice to a lady in a hurry recently. It's not the busiest store in the world. And my luck was in. Someone did remember you."

"And why did they remember me?"

"Because you were carrying a large painting around. To make conversation while you got your money together, she'd asked you what it was. *Catch Me If You Can*, you'd replied, which made her laugh at the time. Call it instinct, call it determination...."

"Or blindingly lucky!" exclaimed Mrs Casey. "Charlie," she continued, looking like she was about to cry, "I was once very poor. I hated it."

"I don't love it, myself."

"No doubt. Look, Jimmy's estate will pay out in a week or so. That means the £50,000 will be mine. All mine. And there's the suitcases full of the blackmail cash. Charlie, I'm rich at last! Very, very, very rich!"

"You won't need it where you're going."

"But Charlie! I could set you up as detective. I could take care of your bills, forever! You could do everything you ever wanted!"

"I want to put criminals away, Mrs Casey. That's all I want."

"Finding my receipt, Charlie... now there's a 'coincidence', wouldn't you agree?" she said bitterly.

Charlie stood up to leave. He still had one question. "Mrs Casey, the police will be here soon. This case is closed. But one thing confuses me. You were home and dry. Jimmy was dead and you were going to inherit all his money. Mortimer would never have told a soul that he had been dealing in stolen goods. So why did you call Hank Kane to investigate? Wasn't that just asking to get caught?"

Mrs Casey looked out of the window and saw the police cars screeching to a halt in front of the house.

She sighed, looked at Charlie and said: "I might as well tell you. You know Mortimer paid Jimmy the blackmail cash, around £250,000, all in three suitcases. Jimmy hid them. I didn't tell you where, because, he never told *me* where! The dirty double-crosser! In fact, Jimmy had cooled on me to say the least. Jimmy was too good at his job. And he'd stopped telling me how his investigation was going. He was close to discovering that it was me who supplied the Gallery with stolen goods.

"So you see, Charlie, Jimmy wised up before he was due to tell me where the suitcases where. And the police wouldn't investigate at first because I'd fixed it to look like an accident. Not even the police noticed the saw marks on the ladder. I'd done too good a job of fixing it so they wouldn't suspect me. No other suspects. No investigation—"

"Just suitcases full of money that you couldn't get your hands on," interrupted Charlie. "I bet it kept you awake; money that no-one could spend."

"You could say that. I heard about Kane Investigations from some really weird guy, some smelly hippy type, who'd approached me in Central Station. Said he'd seen me talking to myself, all distracted. Said I should call his friend who specialised in tracing missing people, and missing 'things'. So I reckoned that was my best bet for

tracking down the blackmail cash in the suitcases –
so I called Mr Kane—"

"And Hank would report all developments on the
case to you, so you'd piece it together before he
would, because you already had a head start."

"Or so I thought. Just tell me, Charlie. Put me out
my misery. Do you know where the money is?"

"I thought I did. But when I got there, it was gone.
Yep, Jimmy did too good a job there. In fact if you
listen carefully, I bet you can hear him laughing now!"

"But, how can that be? The only guys who could
have had any clue to its whereabouts are dead! How
could it go missing?"

"Dunno," replied Charlie. "Coincidence?"

Just then PC Murray came in with some other
policemen. They'd been listening to the whole thing.
Charlie had been wearing a wire the whole time,
which seemed to stop working properly whenever
the suitcases were mentioned. Mrs Casey started
shouting abuse at everyone, telling them that Charlie
had robbed her of suitcases full of money. No-one
seemed to believe her. Who on earth would?

CHAPTER SEVENTEEN

DEAD AGAIN

"ARE you sure this is the right grave?" Charlie whispered to TG He didn't even know why he was whispering as there was no one about.

"I'm sure," he replied, his fetid breath visible in the night air.

It was three o'clock in the morning and Charlie and TG were in the graveyard, spades in hand. Or at least Charlie had his spade in his hand, TG seemed to have taken on the role of foreman.

The night was desperately cold but Charlie wasn't aware of it. He was perspiring, his clothes sticking to him, partly from fear and partly due to exertion.

He continued digging and at last he felt his spade hit something hard. TG shone the torch into the hole that Charlie had painstakingly dug.

"Keep going, Charlie, we're nearly there."

Charlie wiped the sweat from his brow and once again shovelled dirt from the hole. A few more spade fulls and he was almost there. Then came the hard part.

"How are we going to get the coffin out, TG?" he asked.

TG didn't reply. He pushed his cloak back to one side, and moved towards the hole. His body seemed to float over the coffin. Then, with what seemed like superhuman strength to Charlie, TG tore back the lid of the coffin and lifted out the skeletal frame of Hank. He placed the body on the ground beside Charlie.

Charlie was dismayed. How could this possibly be the Hank that he knew? The Hank who made fun of him, called him "Kid", doubted his ability in everything he did? This pile of bones couldn't be the same person, surely?

TG pulled out the bottle with the skull and crossbones on it, from inside his cloak. He poured some of the liquid between the teeth of the skeleton and, before Charlie's very eyes, flesh began to appear. At first he wasn't sure, believing himself to be imagining the whiteness of the skin that seemed to appear on Hank's torso. He looked more closely.

Astonishing! Instead of a skull, Hank's facial features were starting to reappear! Still ugly, but Charlie was delighted! His partner had returned! From the dead! The longer he watched, the more flesh appeared until, eventually, Hank was back.

He and TG stood back, pleased with their work. Hank had been six feet under for so long now that Charlie could only hope they would be forgiven. He also hoped Hank would appreciate the work the two had carried out while he had been absent.

Slowly Hank pulled himself up to a sitting position. His bones creaked as he did so and he shook his head, as though in pain.

He looked, first at TG, then at Charlie.

"Where's my hat?" he grunted.

CHAPTER EIGHTEEN
HANK BACK IN CHARGE

"HANK! You're back! There's so much to tell you!" exclaimed Charlie.

"Look Kid, it was only my body, or should I say, 'my remains' that were buried. My spirit was as free as a bird, only no-one could see me or hear me."

"Except me, Hank," interrupted TG.

"Except you, Grim," replied Hank. "And a few pesky psychics, who threatened to blow my cover."

Charlie looked at both of them in turn. He couldn't believe it! No wonder TG had been so calm about Hank being buried!

"Why didn't you tell me?" he shouted.

"Look, Kid, you solved the case didn't you?" Hank said as he dusted himself down. "Solved it on your own. OK so I provided some clues. But you had to be pretty good to find your way through that kind of maze…."

"Or to have had a damn good guide," interrupted TG once more.

"OK, so TG helped you a little. It was the least he could do."

"Did you help me too Hank?" Charlie hoped that Hank hadn't helped him. It would mean that he'd been a pawn in Hank and TG's crime solving game. A dupe.

"I kept an eye out for you, sure. Help you? Apart from the clues? No. Besides, without my body, there was a limit to what I could do. You really did solve it, Kid. And the way you tore Mrs Casey apart ... well ... that was just thrilling to watch!"

"You were there!"

"Only in my capacity as a ghost! Not as a detective. You are good Charlie, I'll give you that."

Charlie had noticed in their previous adventure how Hank called him 'Charlie', when he was impressed with him. Hank continued,

"But there are a few loose ends here. Let's not be sloppy. Let's see if you solved it all. OK, so the cops are happy. But are we? We shouldn't be. First of all, let's ask some questions. My mysterious intruder, any idea who that was?"

Charlie was going to enjoy this. He'd already answered that one in his head.

"Jimmy Casey," he said with certainty.

CHAPTER NINETEEN

LOOSE ENDS

"BUT he was already dead," protested Hank. Newly dead in fact. How does a dead guy enter my office?"

"You do it every day, Hank, remember? See, I know he was dead, you know he was dead. The only person who didn't know Jimmy was dead was Jimmy himself. I've been reading up on this spooky stuff, except, it isn't really spooky at all. Very logical, in fact. My guess is that when you die, you feel really weird, like you've just woken up. So newly dead Jimmy, feels like he's just fallen out of bed, so what does he start doing? Same thing he did the day before, and the day before that – he keeps on with the investigation that's totally possessed him for months, like some kind of robot – or zombie! That's why he broke into your office."

Hank and TG listened intently. They knew all this of course, but they wanted to see just how much Charlie had worked out for himself.

"Are you guys keeping up with me so far?" asked Charlie with a wicked grin, not unlike the kind Hank often had on his face.

"Don't push it Kid, just keep going," growled Hank.

"Good. OK, so Jimmy knows his wife has asked you to take the case. His spirit is still floating about his house. Because he's dead, his wife doesn't notice him, pretty much like when he was alive really! Anyway, he hears her make the call to you. He snoops about until he finds your address. And because he's dead, he can find your office no problem, it's visible to dead folks, and mere mortals like me as long as we've been invited, otherwise we can't see it."

Charlie suddenly stopped.

"Am I on the right track?" he asked, showing the first trace of doubt.

"So far so good, Kid, but what did Jimmy want from me,?"

"It wasn't money, he left the dollars he found when he could have taken them."

"But he took my wallet."

"Sure he did. He wanted to know who you were, and what you knew."

"About what?"

"About his wife selling the stolen paintings to Mortimer. He was on her trail. He thought maybe you, having taken on the case, might have some proof. He didn't know you'd barely started. After you collapsed in the street, my guess is that Jimmy ran into TG. TG doing the job of any responsible Grim Reaper, appeared to Jimmy. You want to take over from here TG?"

"Hank knows this, Kid, but you are right. What a little smart-ass. Don't get me wrong – we need a smart-ass, one that doesn't need a skull and crossbones magic potion to stay good-looking. Some smart-asses believe it or not, might run outta their office and forget the one thing I told them *never* to forget, huh, Hank!"

"I think that's the eight hundredth time you've reminded me, Grim." Hank looked and felt foolish, a rare occasion indeed.

TG continued: "Jimmy was shocked. He told me it wasn't his time to die yet, that he still had to complete some vital investigation. He was obsessed with it. So, 'Jimmy,' I says to him, 'to save time, here's how it is.' I filled in the blanks for him and then I says, 'investigation complete, comprendez?' Call me heartless but I couldn't resist that. Ha, should've seen the look on his face. What? What do you guys expect from me? I'm the Grim Reaper for crying out loud! I'm not meant to be cute!"

Hank looked at TG, shaking his head. Then he turned to Charlie.

"Just one more thing, Charlie, the suitcases, the ones bursting with cash? Where are they?"

"I thought I knew," said Charlie, for the first time sounding a little lost. "I thought the punchline to all this was that Jimmy Casey, or should I say, his ghost, put them into your office. See, maybe he wasn't breaking into your office to take things *out*. *Maybe* he was putting something *in*. Like, he was storing them there to steal back later. What better place for safe keeping that with the Private Detective his wife hired?

"Jimmy figured that when the detective discovered it, he'd hold on to it till he worked out where it fitted into the investigation. So, this detective won't call the cops, Mrs Casey, or anyone else till he knows exactly what's going on, right? Jimmy, having broken into places for years in his work, reckons he can get it any time, figuring the detective won't risk moving it – not right away anyway. Of course, Jimmy's plan changed a bit when TG pointed out that he was dead!"

Charlie hesitated, but Hank could see that he wanted to say something.

"Go on," encouraged Hank.

Charlie cleared his throat, paused, looked at TG and eventually said, "How's your new suit, TG?"

TG smiled, guiltily.

"'Got it from some dead guy'?" said Charlie. "Really? The latest fashion? I might be a kid, but even I can see when a suit has been worn, or is freshly tailored. It's my job to notice that stuff. You guys always underestimate me, don't you? Makes you sloppy, TG."

"Charles, my dear boy," said TG, still smiling, "Welcome Aboard!" He put his hand out for Charlie to shake. "That money is going straight to the Court of Ghouls. I will personally make sure of it – once I've deducted my expenses, of course."

Charlie ignored the piece about expenses. "What do you mean 'Welcome Aboard'?" he asked.

"You've joined the agency, Kid!" exclaimed the Dead Detective. "Looks like I've got a partner for the first time in my life."

"Can this 'partner' have a name, please, apart from 'Kid'?"

Hank was on the verge of saying "Yep" but instead he just turned away. Charlie could see his shoulders were shaking with suppressed laughter.

CHAPTER TWENTY

BACK IN THE DOCK

HANK was nervous. He was standing outside the courtroom with Charlie and TG by his side.

The court official motioned to the three to go in. The court was now in session. Hank's day of reckoning – again.

The presiding judge barely looked up as Hank entered the courtroom. The other judges looked equally disinterested. The creatures, ghosts and monsters of the jury screeched noisily at one another, some clawing to get at Charlie, unaccustomed to humans being in front of them.

The judge banged the gavel and raised his eyebrows at the Dead Detective..

"Well, Detective Kane? What have you to say in your defence?"

"Defence?" Hank looked offended. "I can't possibly be on trial today, your honour. I've come here to be given a pass to cross over to the other side. Surely you must remember your promise?"

The judge sighed wearily. They'd been through this *so* many times before.

"And you've conducted yourself honourably in this latest case, have you?"

Hank cleared his throat.

"Of course I have, your honour. My conduct has

been excellent. There is no other word to describe it. In fact," he said, looking at his two colleagues, "I have spent the last few weeks being somewhat out of action and my two friends have solved the case on my behalf."

The judge looked weary. "And you didn't offer any help at all to either Mr Christian or The Grim Reaper?"

"No, your honour, how could I? I was absent from the case and played no part in the solving of it other than the three very obscure clues, which I'm sure you'll allow."

The judge looked at Hank and then at Charlie. "And you didn't assist in any way? Any planting of evidence?"

Hank looked uncomfortable.

"Charlie would have got there in the end. He would have *known* the killer was Mortimer. For heaven's sake your honour, credit the kid with some sense. I only tried to…"

The judge once again banged his gavel.

"Guilty, Mr Kane. Case dismissed. See you back here in the not too distant future." He stifled a yawn.

"But your honour…" protested Hank.

The three of them were ushered from the courtroom and the doors banged shut behind them. They found themselves dumped unceremoniously on the street.

Hank shook his head. "Buried alive, so to speak,

for all that time. Believing that when I got out I'd be able to cross over, only to find I'm back where I started."

"Except," the Grim Reaper added, "a little richer!"

"What can I do with money, Grim?"

"I don't mean mere money, Hank. I wouldn't ask you to sully your hands with the stuff. That's a cross I must bear. No, I refer to the fact that you have a partner now. Two heads are better than one – on two different people I mean!"

Hank looked at Charlie. Charlie waited with baited breath. He didn't want to be a partner if Hank didn't think he was up to it. Hank eventually broke into … well … not a smile, but a slight grimace. Still looking at Charlie, he said, "Things could be worse, I suppose." He turned and started the long walk back to his office.

Charlie looked at TG. TG motioned for him to follow Hank while he slipped back into the Court to catch up on some gossip.

The rain had started. Hank pulled up his collar. He shivered, turned round and shouted to Charlie,

"Hey, you'll get soaked. Hurry up, I don't want to catch my death waiting for you."

The two detectives walked towards Buchanan Street precinct, discussing the details of their latest case.

OTHER TITLES IN THE DEAD DETECTIVE SERIES:

DEAD AND UNBURIED

Los Angeles 1953... and Private Detective Hank Kane doesn't know what's hit him. Lying face down on the same street he was just running down, he realises he's been shot. But instead of the morgue, Hank finds himself in the Court of Ghouls, in front of a Vampire judge and a jury of ghosts! He's on trial for cheating on his last case. His punishment? To get back to 'life' and solve a case honestly. Lippy 12-year-old Charlie Christian is assigned as his apprentice detective! The question is not, "will they solve the case?" but "will they solve it honestly?"

DEAD LOSS

Hank gets a visit from the ghost of murder victim Tony Falco, begging for help. Tony, a cat burglar, had stolen jewels on him when he died and the Court of Ghouls won't let Tony into Bandit Heaven until he returns them. Just one problem though – no-one found Falco's body. It's lost! Hank thinks that the Grim Reaper might have some clues. His apprentice, Charlie, is desperate to solve the case without help of any "dead guys", but he disappears! Now the Grim Reaper and Falco have a body full of loot to find – and the apprentice too!

THE CORPSE THAT SANG

A Corpse seen in 1940's Los Angeles turns up in 2002, singing on TV! The strangest coincidence – or is Hank's old flame haunting him. She was a great detective who ended up in Sleuth Heaven – so, why give that up just to sing? Charlie sees the romantic side of Hank and wants to throw up! How can they solve cases with Hank staring at the TV all night? For the first time, Charlie has to take the calls at Hank's office. At last, the Kid can prove his worth, and he resolves to break the case of *The Corpse That Sang*.

THROW AWAY THE KEY

"Help me... please, help me!" A voice identifying itself only as "The Prisoner" keeps calling Hank's phone, pleading for help. Despite being asked why, the panicking voice just keeps calling. Charlie introduces Hank to the latest technology in phone tapping and they listen carefully to the background noises, searching for clues. They get worried when they begin to recognise some sounds, which are too familar for comfort. The Prisoner is very, very close to home!!

GHOST CAR 49

The siren from an old-fashioned American police car is heard echoing around the streets at night. The sound of screeching tyres, blaring police radio, 1940s jazz music and constant gunfire freak out the local residents. Needless to say, Charlie gets the call: " Better get over here, Kid. Looks like we've got something." But how will they bring Car 49 to a halt? And who is at the wheel?!

THE DEAD DETECTIVE SERIES

www.booksnoir.com
www.deaddetective.com

Hey guys! Hank Kane here. Check out my website www.deaddetective.com *to keep up to date with my interactive e-book* Web of Intrigue, *an internet adventure where you, the reader, can help me on the case.*

P.S. You'd better be good!